D0436017

Become a star reader with Caillou!

This three-level reading series is designed for pre-readers or beginning readers and is based on popular Caillou episodes. The books feature common sight words used with limited grammar. Each book also offers a set number of target words. These words are noted in bold print and are presented in a picture dictionary in order to reinforce meaning and expand reading vocabulary.

For pre-readers to read along

- 125-175 words
- Simple sentences
- Simple vocabulary and common sight words
- Picture dictionary teaching 6 target words

For beginning readers to read with support

- 175-250 words
- Longer sentences
- Limited vocabulary and more sight words
- Picture dictionary teaching 8 target words

For improving readers to read on their own or with support

- 250-350 words
- Longer sentences and more complex grammar
- Varied vocabulary and less-common sight words
- Picture dictionary teaching 10 target words

Text: adaptation by Rebecca Klevberg Moeller

Original story written by Sarah Margaret Johanson, based on the animated series CAILLOU
Illustrations: Eric Sévigny, based on the animated series CAILLOU

Chouette Publishing would like to thank the Government of Canada and SODEC for their financial support.

Bibliothèque et Archives nationales du Québec and Library and Archives Canada cataloguing in publication

Moeller, Rebecca Klevberg
Caillou, the sock mystery: read with Caillou, level 2
Previously published as: The missing sock. 2003.
For children aged 3 and up.
ISBN 978-2-89718-449-0

1. Caillou (Fictitious character) - Juvenile literature. 2. Worry in children - Juvenile literature. 3. Lost articles - Juvenile literature. 4. Socks - Juvenile literature. I. Sévigny, Éric. II. Johanson, Sarah Margaret, 1968- . Missing sock. III. Title.

BF723.W67M63 2017 j155.4'1246 C2016-942524-X

Printed in China
10 9 8 7 6 5 4 3 2 1 CHO2004 MAY2017

The Sock Mystery

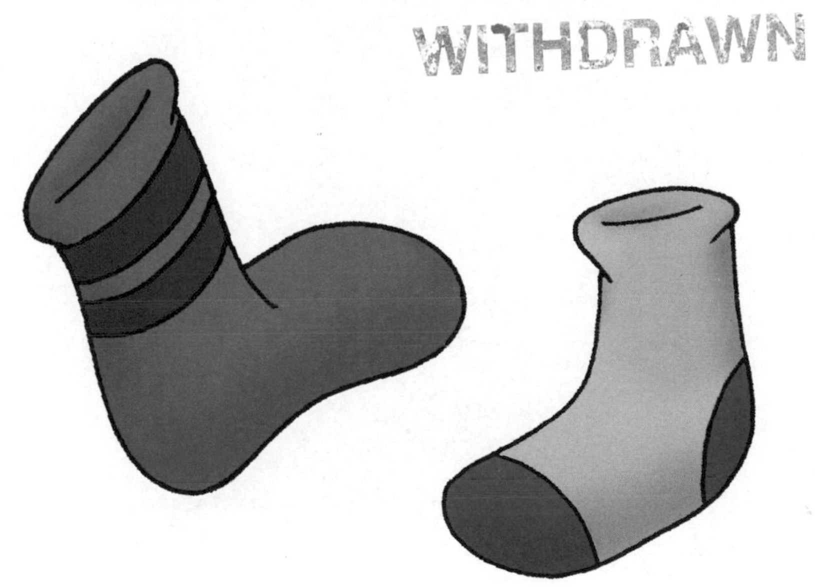

Text: Rebecca Klevberg Moeller, Language Teaching Expert
Illustrations: Eric Sévigny, based on the animated series

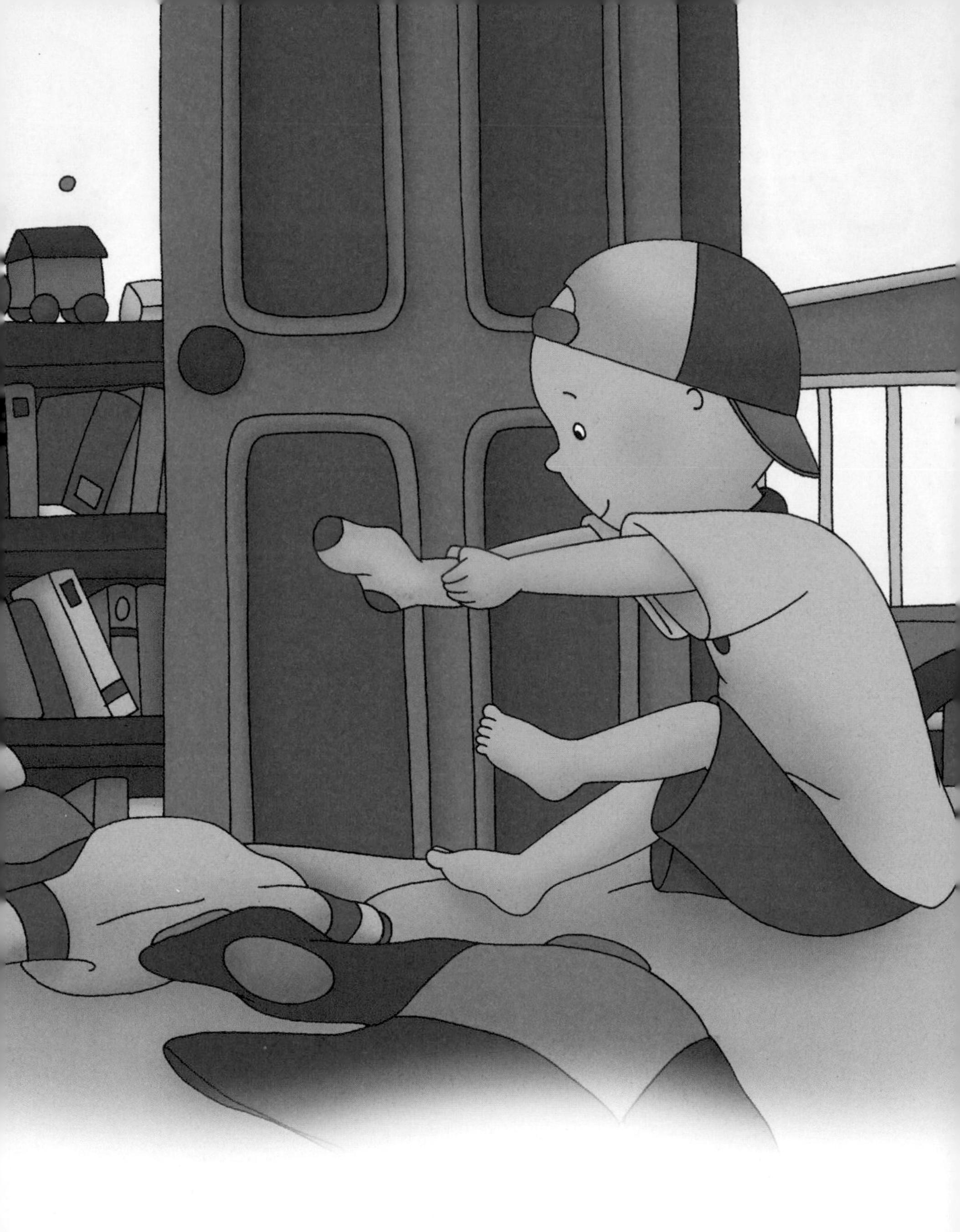

Caillou is getting dressed.

Uh-oh! His **sock** is missing.
It's a mystery!

Caillou goes to the **basement**.
Maybe his **sock** is in the
laundry room.

No **sock** here!

Caillou goes up the **stairs**.

The door is **closed**.
He turns the **doorknob**.

Uh-oh! It's broken!

"Help!" Caillou calls.
"The **doorknob** is broken."
"I'm here!" Daddy says.

Daddy turns the **doorknob**.
The door **opens**. "Hooray!"

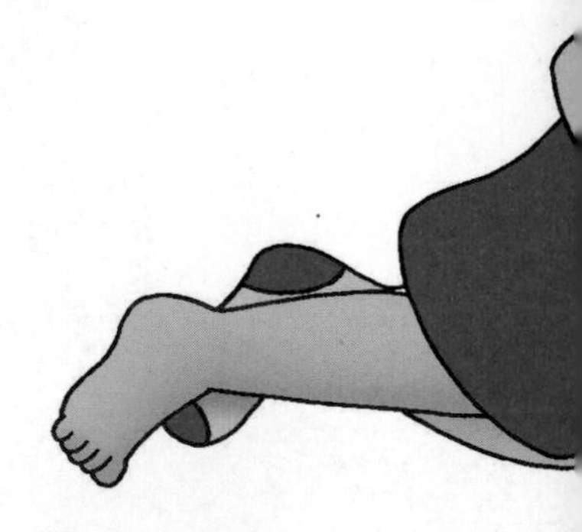

"Why are you in the **basement**?" Daddy asks.
"I'm looking for my **sock**." Caillou answers.
"Let's go look together," Daddy says.

Mommy sees the **open** door.

"Someone could fall in the **stairs**!"
Mommy **closes** the door.

Caillou and Daddy look in
the **laundry room**.
No **sock** in the washer!

No **sock** in the dryer!

"It's OK," Daddy says.

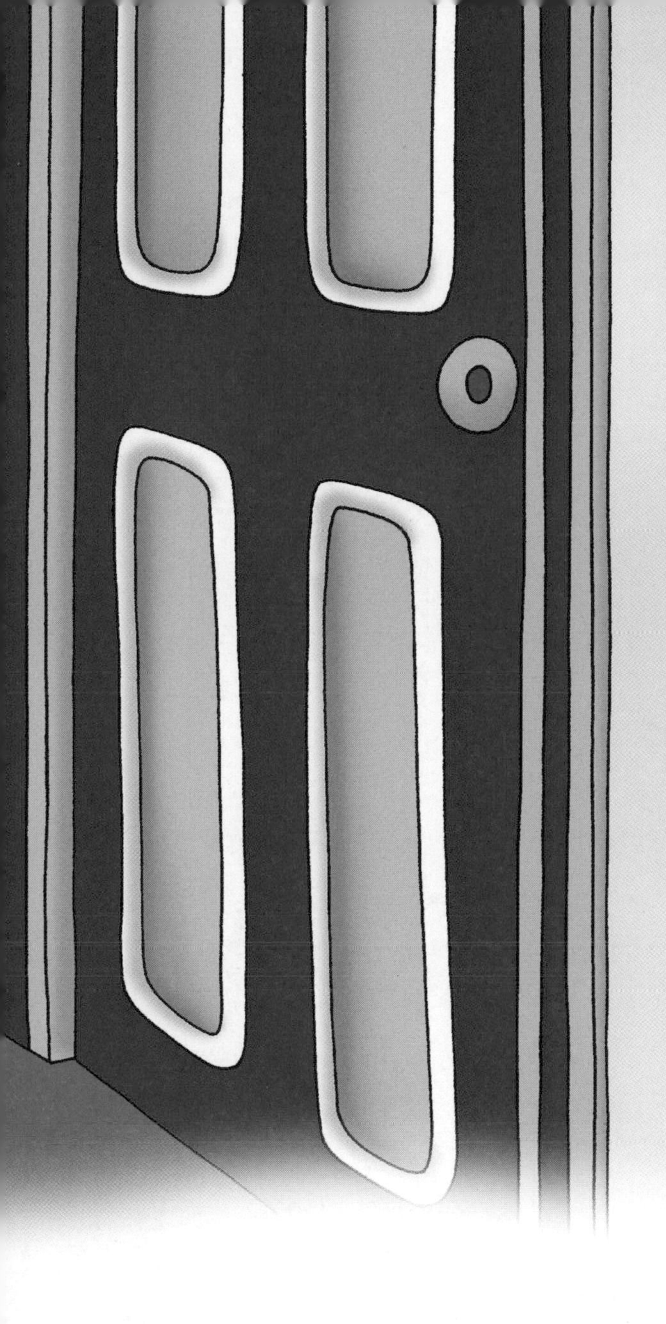

"Let's find new **socks**."

Uh-oh! The **basement** door
is **closed**! They cannot **open** it!
"Help! Help!" they call.

Mommy **opens** the door.
"Are you OK?"
"Yes," Daddy says. "But this **doorknob** is broken. We must fix it!"

Mommy looks down.
"Caillou, where is your
sock?" she asks.

"It's missing. It's a mystery!" Caillou answers.

"Look in the **basket**," Mommy says.
His **sock**!

There is no more mystery.
Now Daddy and Caillou can
fix the **doorknob**!

Picture Dictionary

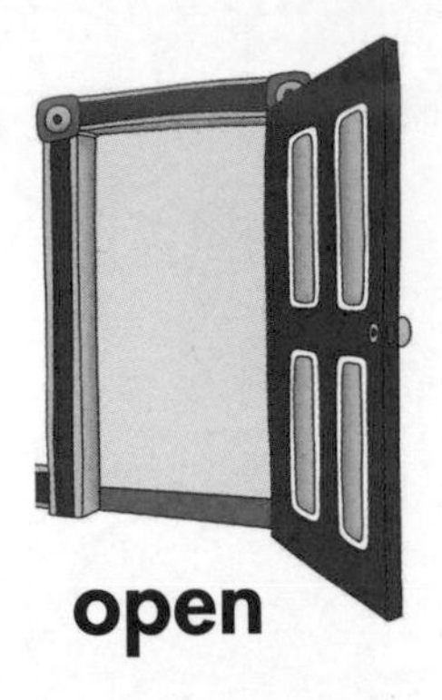

open

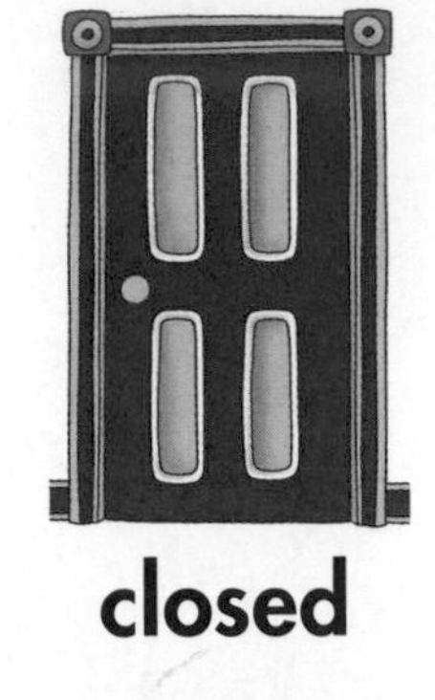

closed

stairs

laundry room

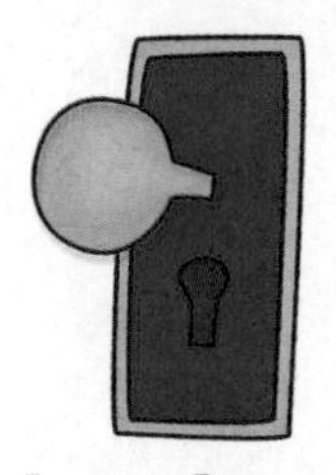

doorknob

basket

sock

basement